Sleepi

Adventures in

Sharon

COPYRIGHT PAGE

Sleeping with the Enemy

Adventures in the Liaden Universe® Number 22

© 2016 by Sharon Lee and Steve Miller

Pinbeam Books

www.pinbeambooks.com

Chimera first published May 2015 on Baen.com

Friend of a Friend is original to this chapbook, published July 2016

ISBN: 978-0-9966346-1-8

Published July 2016 by

Pinbeam Books

PO Box 1586

Waterville ME 04903

email info@pinbeambooks.com

DEDICATION

Virtue is bold
and goodness never fearful
—William Shakespeare
Measure by Measure

A Note From The Author

Characters make fictional worlds go round. They make stories happen, have emotions, make readers read on – and sometimes are more than, or other than, humans. In science fiction and fantasy this "other than human" can be easy to see: robots, raccoons with blasters, turtles with spaceships, mirrors or battle tanks or spaceships who speak up with opinions and special knowledge, trees. . .well, yes, all characters other than human.

There's another set of other than human characters though. There's Trantor, Gehenna, Pern, Dune – yes, those are planets – and the cities of Bellona, Diaspar, and The Dipple, on Korwar.

Science Fiction is full of *place* as character, and we've used it that way ourselves in a number of projects, including the *Low Port* anthology we edited for Meisha Merlin. When place is moody, changeable, and has depth, character is what you're dealing with.

Often, readers don't see place as character, but we're lucky in our readers and over time we've had requests for more about Delgado, or University, or – and this comes to the book you're reading now – Surebleak.

Insofar as Surebleak *is* a character, full of mystery, unfolding new facets all the time, we've had direct requests from readers for "more about Surebleak."

Surebleak is a planet and culture in collision not with one culture but an overwhelming series of cultures – the culture of space travelers, the culture of Scouts, the culture of a galactic Terran community that had been willing to let Surebleak and its population sink from view. And one of the ways those conflicts are best seen is through the way characters, and we mean human characters in this sentence to start, the way characters imbued with Surebleak's character hallmarks, meet the challenge of dealing with those who are not of the world.

"Chimera" – first published on Baen.com in May of 2015 – joins the original story published for the first time here, "Friend of a Friend" in *Sleeping With The Enemy*.

"Friend of a Friend" may feel familiar at first because it, in effect, began in *Dragon in Exile* and you'll find some portion of it there. But "Friend. . ." wouldn't have fit in *Dragon In Exile* as that book developed, and so it was written more as a "what-if" or a "it could have happened" rather than being a mere outtake from a novel.

We hope you'll enjoy and let your friends know that Surebleak is a character, and a recurring one at that. You'll be seeing more as time goes on.

—Steve Miller
Cat Farm and Confusion Factory
July 15, 2016

Chimera

There'd been a lot of shouting at that meeting—well, there always *was* shouting at the meetings Farnch took him to. Wasn't no use saying he didn't wanna go, on account the shouting hurt his head—Farnch just called him an auntie, and shoved him into the nearest wall. Then Jewl would yell, and punch Farnch, too, if he wasn't faster'n her fist, which wasn't *nobody* faster'n Jewl's fist—and Farnch'd get mad, but even Farnch knew better'n to swing on Jewl, so he'd just get madder'n madder, 'til Darby's head was like to bust with it, and either Farnch'd go out with his crew, or Darby'd go up to the garden 'til either he could hear himself think, or the tips of his ears started to burn in the cold, or Jewl sent one of the twins up to bring him back inside.

Jewl'd been feelin' bad these last couple days, and he'd just managed to get her to sleep when Farnch'd come home, growling about how there was a meeting and it was up to him and Darby help take Surebleak back. . .and all the other kind o'nonsense Farnch was on about lately, him having a grudge against the New Bosses. Farnch, he'd been ambitious, under the Old Bosses. He'd been working all the angles there was, and some that, in Darby's personal opinion, didn't really exist, looking to get onto Boss Goyan's staff. Farnch's big plan was to work his way up to insurance man.

He'd've prolly made, too, Farnch being just that mean, but then what should happen but Boss Conrad come to Surebleak, just particularly to ruin Farnch's life. Least, that's the way Farnch felt about it, and there wasn't any way at all that Darby could change what his brother felt about having his life-plan ruined.

So, for the sake of Jewl's rest, and his own fragile head, Darby'd come along quiet to the meeting, and sat through the yelling and the hating, and the wanting to do something-or-someone a lot of hurt and harm.

That last, that was the worst. He could mostly ignore the yelling and the hating. . .well, that wasn't so bad when there were lots of folks. The feeling got. . .spread out, somehow. Hate was a lot harder to deal with, when it was concentrated in one person.

The bloodlust, though, that got scarier'n a sleet-storm, real fast. Killing rage multiplied in a crowd, until it overwhelmed every sane thought in the room.

Hadn't been so bad tonight; tonight being a planning meeting. There was gonna be a shooting competition at Sherman's, and all the New Bosses were gonna be there with their 'hands. The Streeters for Taking Back Surebleak committee—that was what Farnch's friends called themselves, though Darby didn't see that Surebleak'd gone anywhere. Sure, there was the new people come in—Liadens and suchlike—but *Surebleak* was still right there under the boots where it'd always been, far's Darby knew about it. . .

Anyhow, the Streeters for Surebleak, they was thinking maybe to disrupt that shoot, and show the New Bosses a thing or three, and put the fear of winter into 'em.

So that was the meeting, and he'd lasted 'til it was over, pretty well pleased to've come out in good order, with only the tiniest headache, and his ears ringing with the shouting.

"Darb, we're going on down to Rogin's and talk about this some more. You coming?"

No, no. He knew '*way* better'n drinkin' with Farnch and his friends and talking some more about real 'bleakers and how the foreigners had taken every good thing that'd ever been in everybody's hand, like they'd forgotten the way it *had* been, with the Old Bosses.

Like they'd *liked* the way it'd been, under the Old Bosses.

Well, and that was just it. The way he'd understood it, the couple times he couldn't think of an excuse not to go with Farnch's crew, was they *had* liked the old ways better. They were strong, and liked violence, too—that was the difference between them and Darby. He could hold his own in a fight—wouldn't lived long on the streets after their dad died, if he hadn't learned that. Wasn't as fast as Jewl, nor not as big as Farnch, but he was quick, and he knew where to hit.

Didn't like to fight, that was all. 'specially didn't like to fight when there wasn't anything to fight *about*.

Farnch, though—was waiting for an answer, and Darby was walking the thin line of making him look bad in front of his crew.

"Can't tonight," he said, managing to sound like he felt sad about that. "Gotta check on Jewl; see if she's any better."

"Right," said Farnch, who'd been pretty put out with having to make his supper outta twin-made soup and a handwich. "Tell 'er I expect to see her fresh as a new fall tomorra."

Jewl wasn't likely to be up tomorrow, but there wasn't any use telling Farnch that. Always worked out better with Farnch, if he just discovered things when they happened, 'stead of giving him to time to work up a mad.

So.

"I'll tell her," Darby said, and nodded to his brother's crew before he headed on down the street.

"Brother ain't real keen?" he heard Vesti ask. It'd *be* Vesti. Always making trouble, that girl.

"He's in," Farnch said, his voice getting thinner as the crew headed off in the opposite direction. "No doubt there. M'sister's been sick, is all, and he worries over her like she was our ma."

In point of actual fact, Darby didn't remember their ma all that sharp; she'd already been sick when he'd come along. Jewl'd been there from the first; Jewl'd had the raising of him, Jewl and Dad, 'til Dad got made a zample. Jewl'd got pregnant right after—'nother kind of zample-making, which was something he wasn't s'posed to know, and Jewl didn't never talk about. That got 'em the twins, and Jewl'd been first-minded to toss 'em out into the snow. He'd worked with her on that, just putting weight and warm on what Gran Delaros said when she come to check in, which she'd done three, five times a day, at first, when Jewl wouldn't get up, and turned her face into the pillow when the twins was brought to suck. It took some time, it took some work, but the talk about snowbanks melted away, and she'd cuddle 'em a little when they nursed, and started in to play with 'em, and to pick 'em up, instead of leaving that to Darby or to Gran—Farnch, he'd been out with his crew, mostly, 'round then, him needing to stablish his space on the sidewalk. . .

"Alien! I'm gonna stomp you inta paste you little—"

The voice was loud, and slurred, coming from the street on Darby's left. There was the sound of meat hitting meat, and a soft cry, then another yell—and Darby was running, not *away* from the fight, which woulda been sensible, but *toward* it.

#

Darby recognized the big guy—Pablo Gerstein, who'd been Boss Goyan's insurance man—the guy Farnch'd planned to throw outta his job. Now Goyan'd gotten retired, Pablo, he'd kinda retired, too, bullying the local bartenders into giving him drinks, and staying just a little drunk, and a lot belligerent, all the time.

Nowadays, he got his money by beating up 'streeters less able with their fists, or less willing to give—or take—damage, than he was.

Tonight, he had his mark pushed up into a corner—Darby had a fast glimpse of a short, slender figure, ducking not quite out of the way of Pablo's fist, and then he was on it, grabbing the big man by the elbow, and spinning him around with a yell.

"You bastid!" Pablo shouted. "Better get the sleet outta here, or I'll—"

Darby swung, taking advantage of the big man's chancy balance, to land a good one on his jaw.

That sent him staggering, but punches weren't the way to take Pablo down. Even a hard strike to the skull didn't always do the trick; years of drinking had given him a head as hard as a paving stone.

The big man'd already recovered, and was coming in swinging with his ham fists. Darby ducked inside the other's reach, got a good chest punch in, and turned his head to yell at the mark, who was still standing in that corner.

"Run!"

Well, that was a mistake. Pablo's fist came outta nowhere, and the next thing Darby was seeing was snowflakes, in real pretty colors, and feeling the wall against his back.

Pablo was so mad, he didn't have any more words; he was still fighting, though—roaring, too—and all his attention on Darby.

Desperately, Darby pushed himself away from the wall—and there was a flash of motion between him and Pablo, a short, slight figure that seemed to skate over the surface of the street, hand striking high, foot striking low. Darby heard something go crunch, Pablo screamed and—fell over.

"Sleet and thunder!" Darby yelled. He dashed forward, grabbed the little guy by the arm and dragged him in his wake.

"C'mon! Run while he's down!"

#

Half a block away, Darby felt the little guy kind of stagger under his hand, and caught a spike of pain. He slowed, shifting his grip to give the boy some support under the elbow.

"Hey," he said, breathless, "you OK?"

The street was dark, but there was a little spill from the sign over Greenlie's Dry Goods, enough to see a thin face behind a long snarl of reddish brown hair, bruises already rising along a high, fragile cheek. Dark eyes looked at him straightly, brows pulled against that little burn of pain.

"You OK?" Darby asked again. "My place is just another block down. Can you walk that far? I don't think Pablo's gonna be chasing after us. That knee must hurt where you kicked him."

"Indeed," the voice was light, and somewhat unsteady. "If I re-membered my. . .lessons, that knee. . .cap is crushed. Pablo will re-quire a physician."

Something flickered over his face—another sort of pain, Darby caught—and that fast, it was gone.

"I am Kez Rel ter'Ista Clan Wilkin," he said. "I thank you for your. . .timely assistance." He paused, and Darby felt the shiver go through him. "What is your name, sir?"

"Darby Bajek, and I ain't a sir. Just Darby's good. You OK to walk down to my place?"

"There is no need for you to trouble yourself further. I will continue to my lodgings."

Darby eyed him, seeing the wobble in the knees, and feeling the flicker of pain, and something else, *around* the pain. He wanted a closer look at that, but first things first. The boy needed to sit down and collect himself, else he was gonna fall over onto his pointy little nose.

"'less your lodging's right next door here, you're better coming with me. Get you cleaned up, something to settle you—my nephew made a big pot o'soup for our supper. Sure was good, and I'm betting there's still a cup left for you. While you're having that, we'll get you a taxi to the lodging."

Darby paused, considering. He didn't get the feeling that Kestrel Terista was afraid; *sensibly wary* maybe covered it. Still, couldn't hurt to say it out, plain.

"Won't hurt you."

He heard the sharp intake of breath, saw the eyes widen, maybe in insult—and then a wry smile.

"Thank you. . .Darby. I will come with you, and call a taxi."

"That's the ticket. Just right this way."

He thought about offering an arm to lean on, remembered that half-gasp of insult and bit his tongue. He did set a slow pace, though, down the street, toward home.

#

Ean opened up a crack, took Kestrel Terista in with one wide blue stare, and stepped back to fling the door open.

"Farnch?" he asked, when they were inside, and he had pushed the door to, but not locked it, yet.

"Down Rogin's with the crew," Darby told him. "This is Kestrel Terista, E. He got on Pablo's bad side. Kestrel, this is my nephew, Ean, E for short. He'll show you where to get cleaned up."

There was a weighted silence from his side, and he turned to look at his guest. The right side of his face was swollen and starting to go purple; his eye just a dark slit. The left side showed smooth, gold-colored skin, and a well-opened dark brown eye, just at the moment staring right at him.

Darby concentrated, and caught something like humor and aggravation twisted around together, 'til it was hard to feel one from t'other.

"If I done something wrong, you're gonna hafta tell me what it was so I can make it right," he said. "Only thing I can say is, I don't mean to offend. We're maybe not quite what you're used to, here."

Humor bloomed, and the thin mouth curved slightly upward.

"That is very true—for both of us, I think. Thank you for your care, Darby. I am pleased to meet your nephew." He inclined his head, carefully, as Darby read it, in E's direction.

"Was it you who made the supper-soup?"

"Nah, that was Peor. I made the handwiches." Ean cocked his head to one side. "We got some o'both left over, if you need something to eat, after you wash your face."

"Thank you. A cup of soup would be. . .welcome."

"'k, then. C'mon this way, so you can wash up. . ." E led Kestrel down the hall toward the lav.

Peor came in from the kitchen side, looking worried.

"How's Jewl?" Darby asked.

Peor's worry was like a snowfog, clammy and chill.

"She was cold, and wanted another blanket," he said. "I brought her the one off our bed, but she was still cold, so I got your blanket, too, and our winter coats." He took a breath.

"We tried to get her to eat some soup, but she didn't want it. E got 'er to drink some warm water, and then she said her head hurt. I sat with 'er while E did his schoolwork. He came to switch out with me when she was just back asleep. We looked in a couple times, but she was still sleeping."

Darby shivered; felt Peor's worry spike.

"You did good," Darby said, and smiled. "I'll go check on her now. You hear we got a visitor?"

Peor nodded. "We still got plenty dinner, like E said. Darb?"

"Yeah."

"Is Kestrel Liaden?"

"Pretty sure so, why?"

"Maybe better get him outta here 'fore Farnch comes home?"

Before Farnch came home after a full night drinking with his friends, and telling over all the wrongs that Liadens had put onto them.

"Yeah. Whyn't you zip down to Miz Prestoro's and call for a taxi? Oughta be here by the time he finishes his soup."

"All right," Peor said. And, "Is Ma gonna be all right, Darb? She was. . .she was crying, that's how cold she was."

Jewl never cried. *Never*. Not even the night she come home beat up and bleeding and all her nails and a couple fingers broke.

Darby controlled his own shiver, and gave Peor a nod.

"I'll go in and check on her. You two take care of Kestrel."

Peor nodded.

Darby went down the hall, to his sister's room.

He eased the door open, so's not to wake her, if she was still sleeping. The lamp was on in the corner, with a towel thrown over it to dim the glare and to ease Jewl's aching head.

He didn't see her, at first, just the pile of blankets and winter coats in the center of the bed. Then he saw a movement, as his eyes adjusted—a tiny constant movement of that mountain of cloth.

Shivering.

He crossed the room and knelt by her bed, reaching beneath the blankets to find her, the while feeling. . .feeling. . .

. . .absent, cold, so cold, and all his thought was focused on how to get her warm, if this wasn't enough.

His questing hand found hers, like ice.

A sound—a *whimper*—and he'd've never in his whole life heard Jewl make any such sound.

Carefully, he peeled back the edge of the blankets until he found her face, flushed, and damp, and when he put his hand across her forehead, burning hot.

There was a fever going 'round; Mister Warchiski, who worked at the clinic, he'd told him about it, two, three weeks ago.

"Summer flu," Mister Warchiski'd said, and added, like an afterthought, "nasty one."

Darby stroked Jewl's hair back from her face; it was soaked, like she'd just come outta the shower.

He needed help, he thought carefully, *Jewl* needed help. Clinic—but he didn't want to move her, sick as she was and maybe infectious, too. Call, then. Maybe the clinic had a traveling doctor.

Darby got to his feet, pulled the covers back over his sister, and left her, moving fast. Kitchen first, where Kestrel sat at their table, clean and neat, his hair combed and braided, and tied off with a piece of twine. There was still that little hot-spot of pain, wound around with whatever it was, but Darby didn't have time for that now.

"Kestrel, you gotta go," he said, which was maybe too abrupt, but there was Jewl back there in bed, freezing and burning at the same time.

Kestrel raised his head, and gave him a sharp look out of his one open eye.

"Immediately?" he asked.

"That's it. Maybe Miz Prestoro'll let you wait for the taxi at her place. Peor went down to call it, so it shouldn't be long. But you gotta go now. I'm real sorry, but my sister's sick, worse'n I thought."

Kestrel put the cup down, and rose from the table.

"Take me to her," he said, briskly.

Darby shook his head.

"Not smart. She's gotta fever; prolly contagious."

"Yes, that's very possible. However, I may be able to help."

Darby blinked at him, seeing E sitting stiff at the table, his face white and his eyes wide.

"Help? How can you help?"

Kestrel was seen to sigh.

"I am a physician," he said, and stepped around the table, reaching out to pick up his jacket as he came.

"Please. Take me to your sister."

#

Kestrel had taken an instrument case from inside his jacket, and opened it on the table next to Jewl's bed. He took a long moment to examine each object, his tension palpable, but not overstrong. Likewise, his relief upon finding his instruments undamaged was perfectly clear, without being overwhelming.

"Please, if you will pull the blankets back?" Kestrel said. "I would not wish to distress her with a stranger's touch, when she has kin by her."

"Sure."

Darby came to the opposite side of the bed, and eased the covers back, until he'd uncovered her to the waist. Her face was white, with fire-red splotches high on her cheekbones; her hair was a soggy snarl across the pillow.

"Enough," murmured Kestrel. "Hold her hand, and sit, so she will see you, if she should wake."

Darby sat on the bed and took his sister's hand, twining their fingers together as he felt for her—but all he got was a sort of vast weariness.

"I don't think she'll wake up," he told Kestrel. "She's just. . .really tired."

"Thank you. Please tell me if that state alters. I will now take her measurements—blood pressure, temperature, respiration."

Ean and Peor were watching from the door, so tense that Darby felt he might start crying himself. He tried not to pay attention; focusing his concentration on Jewl.

Concentration and calm—that was what spilled from Kestrel, like a cool, bracing breeze. Darby breathed in some of that cool competence, and felt it settle his nerves, while the examination proceeded.

"How does she fare? Is she wakeful?"

"No. . .'bout the same. Just. . .too tired even to dream."

Kestrel sighed, and turned back to his case.

"As you know, she—what is her name, your sister?"

"Jewl."

"Jewl," he repeated, like he was tasting the sound. "Jewl has a high fever; her blood pressure is elevated; her white blood count is elevated. These things indicate that she is fighting an infection."

"The summer flu," Darby said.

"That is how they name it at the clinic, yes. Now, I have something—a small injection—that will bring the fever to a less dangerous level. She will rest easier. I would not disturb her tonight. Tomorrow, she must be taken to the clinic, so that she may be more thoroughly diagnosed and treated. Call, and they will send the clinic taxi, so that the opportunity for infecting others is lessened. Do you understand this? I wish to be clear."

"Understood," Darby said.

"Good. I will administer the injection." He did that, and returned the injector and the rest of his instruments to the case.

"Someone ought to stay with her," he said, slowly. "If she wakes and asks for food, she may take some of Peor's good soup. Tea, or water—warm, or tepid, not cold." He sighed again, and seemed to sag where he stood. Darby felt a wave of pain-laced weariness flow from him, and, unthinking, reach out to ease the pain, and instill a little burst of energy.

Kestrel looked up, lips parted, as if he were going to say something.

But whatever he was about to say was cut off by the sound of the door opening, and a heavy, uncertain tread in the main room.

"Hey!" Farnch called, voice slurred. "Where's everybody?"

#

Peor and Ean ran out, meaning, so Darby felt, to turn Farch toward the kitchen.

"Put on your jacket," Darby said to Kestrel, as he got up from Jewl's bed, and pulled the covers back up to cover her shoulders.

"Stay behind me. Sounds like my brother had one beer too many. Gets feisty. I'll take you down to Miz Prestoro's. Taxi oughta been here by now."

"Sleet, no, I don' wanany o'that slop. I want real food. Where's Jewl? In bed already? Get 'er up and tell 'er I gotta have something to eat."

"Ma's sick," Peor said, voice shrill with worry. "She's gotta sleep."

"Sick, is it? She can go back to bed after she gets me something to eat."

It wasn't cool competence Kestrel was feeling now; it was outright alarm, though not, as Darby parsed it, for himself. He was worried for his patient.

Darby wanted to tell him that they'd settle Farch, and keep him away from Jewl, but there was the main room coming up, and the door, and Farch just to one side of it, listing a little as he yelled at Peor.

Darby took a breath, and walked firmly toward the door.

Farch spun, staggered, caught sight of Kestrel, and froze.

"Liaden," he said, flat-voiced and suddenly sounding stone sober.

Darby stopped, keeping his body between Kestrel and his brother.

"Liaden," Farch said again, and lurched one step forward, roaring fit to wake al the neighbors.

"You cow-eyed auntie! Screwing a sleet-scarred Liaden in my own house? Or, no, wait—it's Jewl, ain't it? Sleeping, is she? I'll damnwell make sure she's *sleeping*!"

He lunged, and Darby felt his brother's intent to strike out, at him, at Kestrel, and Jewl—and that intention of his brother's, it...set fire to something inside him. He didn't know what it was, and he sure didn't know what to do with it...

...except to strike out, and strike down, and stop Farnch *right now*!

Fire seared through him. He saw his brother stagger, and crumble to his knees, before his own sight went grey, then black, and he hit the floor hard.

#

A sharp smell filled his head, and he sat up, choking, his eyes running with tears. Through them, he could see Kestrel, kneeling beside him.

"See, there," he said, to the twins, who were leaning over his shoulders. "He is well, your Uncle Darby. He may have a headache. I understand that this is sometimes a result of such strikes, but he will do very well."

Darby sat up, looking into Kestrel's one good eye, but reading nothing there. The cool flow of calmness was back, wonderfully bracing.

"Farnch?" he said, his voice hoarse, and his head still filled with the stinging scent.

"Most soundly asleep," Kestrel said promptly. "I detected no harm done. I would suggest that he be left where he is until he wakes."

He used his chin to point to the left. Darby looked, and there was Farnch, stretched out full length on his back, snoring away.

He looked back to the twins.

"Getcher Uncle Farnch a blanket, right?"

"Right," E said, and ran down the hall to Farnch's room, and the only bed in the house that hadn't given its blankets to Jewl.

Kestrel sat back on his heels, and stowed the little vial inside his jacket.

"I would like to talk with you," Kestrel said, "when we have both rested and recovered." He had a card between his fingers; and held it out. Darby took it, gingerly, never taking his eyes from Kestrel's tired, bruised face.

"Call me, please, and let us meet for tea and—and *chernubia*—" a wry smile. "See how I am tired? I lose my Terran. I mean. . .*dessert*. Will you do this?"

"Yes," Darby said. "I'll do that."

"Good." Kestrel stood, and leaned down, offering a wiry hand.

Darby took it and climbed inelegantly to his feet.

"You should find your bed," Kestrel said. "My friend Peor has offered his escort to Ms. Prestoro."

"All right," Darby said. He felt slow, and stupid, and out on his feet. "Good-night."

"Good-night," Kestrel said, and followed Peor out the door.

Darby stood there, feeling blank, until E came back with a blanket and threw it over Farnch.

"You better hit the bed," he said, looking at Darby critically. "Peor an' me'll watch Ma."

He nodded.

"If she looks like getting worse, you call me," he said.

"Deal," said Ean, and Darby nodded again, and walked unsteadily down the hall to his bed.

\#

Ander's Sweet Shop was just a block away from the clinic, and in the not-so-far-away past he'd've had to pay a toll to get across that street, if the tollkeepers let him through at all, which wasn't that certain a thing, Boss Goyan and Boss Rinehart not bein' what you'd call best friends.

Today, it was just zackly as easy as crossing the empty street—empty 'cause almost everybody'd gone to the big shootout at Sherman's—and walking down to the door under the bright yellow awning.

Darby walked slow, trying to get himself in order, though why he should be in *dis*order was a puzzle all its own. He wanted to see Kestrel again—it'd been seven days since the night they'd met. Jewl was up again, good as ever she'd been. Good enough to fight with Farnch about sending the twins to the new consolidated school.

That was an argument came 'round every time it snowed, seemed like, and Farnch wouldn't allow it, him being head of the family. This time, though, Jewl'd said that she'd found rooms to let, affordable, nearer to her work *and* to the school, and she figured Farnch'd do just fine as the head of a household of one.

Jewl was good enough at her numbers that Darby figured she meant him to go with her, which. . .wasn't as warming as it might've been on another day.

Funny thing about that argument, though—Jewl'd won. Farnch got to the point where usually he punched the wall, or threw something or—and it was like the mad went right outta him, and he just shrugged and said if she wanted to get her brats mixed up with the New Bosses, it was all on her, whatever happened.

Why he was thinking about that now, Darby didn't zackly know, 'cept prolly Kestrel would want to know how his patient was. He figured that was it, and he took a good hard breath before he pushed open the door, and stepped into the sweet shop.

Smells hit him first—chocolate, cinnamon, vanilla—and he paused for a second, just to let his nose get its fill. Then, he looked around the room. There ahead of him was the counter, all sorts of good things on display. To his left, there were a couple of tables, and a short, slim man wearing a brown jacket over a winter-weight blue sweater, was standing up from a table for three, while a dark-haired woman remained seated, watching him with interest.

The man came forward, reddish brown braid falling forward over his shoulder, and it was right then that he recognized Kestrel, his face smooth and unbruised, both eyes wide open. A waft of cool amusement reached him, and he smiled.

"Almost din't recognize you," Darby said, walking forward with his hand out, "with all them bruises gone."

Kestrel hesitated, then placed his hand into Darby's, but not like he was going to shake. Instead, he brought Darby forward, to the table, and the woman waiting there.

"I hope you will forgive me for bringing a. . .friend with me," he murmured. "I think you may find her of use."

"Of use?" Darby asked, but Kestrel had let go of his hand, and gave the woman a heavy nod of head.

"Hestya, this is the young man I told you of—Darby Bajek. Darby, this is Hestya van'Lorin. She is a colleague from the clinic."

Another doctor then, Darby thought, and gave her a friendly nod.

"Pleased to meet you, ma'am."

"And I am pleased to meet you, Darby Bajek." Her voice was. . .harder than Kestrel's, her accent more pronounced. And the feelings he got from her—well, he didn't get *any* feelings from her. None at all.

She smiled.

"Aha! I confuse him!" she said, like it was a pretty good joke. She raised a hand and waved at the two vacant chairs. "Please, sit. I refuse to strain my neck by looking up at you."

They sat, and Kestrel waved to the guy behind the counter.

"Tea will come," he said, settling into his chair, "and a selection of sweets."

"Kez Rel tells me that we may share a gift, you and I," Hestya said, then, leaning forward with her elbows crossed onto the tabletop.

Darby blinked, at her accent, and suddenly turned toward Kestrel—toward *Kez Rel* —his ears burning.

"No wonder you were mad!" he blurted. "I got your name wrong! You shoulda told me."

"Well, and so I should have," *Kez Rel* said, and put a hand on Darby's wrist. "But, I found I liked the error. *Kestrel*. And, truly, panting as I was, and my face in such a state, it was wonderful that you made a guess that was anything so close. Please, I would be honored if you would continue as you have begun. I will have a *nickname*—do I have that correctly?"

"That's right," Darby said, doubtfully. "If you're sure you don't mind."

"Not at all," Kestrel told him, and looked up as the tray arrived with tea and a plate of sweet things.

#

"So," Hestya said, after they had each sipped some tea, and chosen a sweet. "Darby—I may call you Darby?"

"Yes, ma'am."

"Excellent. I will be Hestya, and Kez Rel will be Kestrel—a tidy band of mischief-makers, eh?"

Darby felt a flicker of amusement from Kestrel, but still nothing from Hestya, though she was clearly teasing.

She smiled, and raised her tea cup.

"I see that I remain a cipher. Would you like to learn to be so mysterious yourself, Darby?"

He frowned.

"I don't think I understand you, m—Hestya."

"I think that you half-understand me," she chided him; "but allow it to stand. Tell me, how fares your brother?"

"My—brother?"

"Indeed. His name is, perhaps. . .Farnch? Kestrel tells me that you felled him with a thought on the adventure-filled night of your meeting."

Darby looked down into his teacup, then up to meet Hestya's eyes. They were light blue. He felt concern, from Kestrel, and remembered the night of their meeting and the way he had controlled his pain. He thought Hestya had taught him that, and wondered if she'd teach him. But, he had a shrewd hunch that she wouldn't teach him anything until he gave her an answer.

"My brother Farnch is doing pretty well, thank you."

Hestya inclined her head.

"No headaches? Noooo. . . *behaviors* that are, for him, not quite what you might expect?"

"Well, no, he—"

He stopped, remembering the fight with Jewl, and how Farnch'd just given up.

"There is something," Hestya said, softly. "Tell me."

"He—it's just he let my sister win an argument. Old argument, 'bout whether or not the twins oughta go to the school. Got to the place where usually he throws something, and he just kinda...folded up. All the temper went right out o'him and he told her to do what she wanted, and remember that if something happened, it was her fault."

"Ah. And this is new, since you struck him?"

"I didn't—*strike*—him," he said hotly. "I only—only—"

He floundered to a stop. Hestya was watching him with interest, her head tipped to one side.

"Yes, I see," she said, when he just sat there like a lump and his face burning. "You have not the words, and it sounds foolish—to you—to say that you pushed your brother with your anger. Was it something like this?"

He felt a hard shove at his—at *him,* dammit! At where he lived, in the center of his head. He threw up a hand, even though he knew that wouldn't stop what she'd thrown at him.

Across from him, Hestya threw her hand up, too, reflecting him. The pressure...stopped.

Darby cleared his throat.

"I guess it must've felt sorta like that—to Farnch," he said slowly. "To me, it felt like—it felt like I...caught fire, and threw it all at him. He was gonna—he was drunk, and he was gonna hurt somebody." He threw an apologetic glance at Kestrel.

"My brother don't much like Liadens. He's got...politics."

Kestrel inclined his head, but it was Hestya who spoke.

"We have been told that there are no Terran Healers," she said. "This would appear to be...an error. Clearly, you are a Healer, Darby Bajek, as I am. The difference between us is that I have been taught control, which makes it much more unlikely that I would unintentionally kill my brother."

"Kill!" he stared at her, his breath gone like she'd punched him. He felt Kestrel's hand on his wrist again, and a waft of gentle concern.

"Kill," Hestya said. "Your gift is no shy flower, my friend; if I were not shielded, I don't doubt you would deafen me. But there is more. Kestrel tells me that you gave him peace and strength when his energy was flagging. Is that true?"

"Yeah. He was out on his feet, and he still had to get home. Little jig o'energy was all; didn't hurt anything."

"Indeed, it was precisely what was needed, as I understand the case. However. A Healer does not Heal, unasked. There are...ethical considerations."

Darby looked down at his tea cup, picked it up and drank, deeply. When he put the cup back on the table, Kestrel refilled it from the pot.

"I didn't know that," he said. "I'm sorry, Kestrel. I hope I didn't hurt you."

"No harm," Kestrel assured him, with his slight smile.

"One could not expect you to know," Hestya said in her hard voice. "You have had no training, and you are, therefore, a—what is the phrase, here? Ah! You are *a danger on the street*, Darby Bajek. You must be less than that—and more."

"You'll teach me?" he asked.

She threw up both hands in a wide gesture, the meaning of which was lost on him.

"It would seem so. I will not be your only teacher. There is a Hall here—a poor thing, compared to the Great Hall at Solcintra, but we will do our duty by our kindred."

"I can't pay," he said, thinking that was prolly rude, but also that she had to know that, right off. "Maybe teach me just to do what you're doing—or what Kestrel did, when he was hurting, and needed not to be distracted by it."

A flash of shrewd blue eyes.

"Ah, you saw that, did you? Well. I think you are very much worth our time, Darby Bajek. We will teach you. When you have learned all that you may, then we will discuss proper payments, and Balance."

Darby glanced to Kestrel.

"Are you a. . .Healer, too?"

"I? No, I am. . .sensitive. I may learn such things as the small wall, to separate and control. . .distress. And I am aware of a Healer's touch." He looked to Hestya.

"Will you have him in the Hall?" he asked. "Or with us?"

She held her cup out, and he poured tea for her, while she studied Darby through half-closed eyes.

"The Hall," she said, after she had taken a sip from her newly filled cup. "He must learn to be safe, first."

Kestrel inclined his head; and raised it to smile at Darby.

"The Healers will teach you, and you will be able to teach others. Also, we would like to woo you. Or, at least, *I* would like to woo you. Hestya must, of course, bide by her *melant'i* as teacher, first."

Woo. . .

That got a body warm and thinking about things he hadn't thought about since Sandep started seeing his other boy, and then lied about it when Darby'd asked him—like Darby couldn't see a lie two blocks distant.

But, there'd been something else—a word. Words were, in Darby's experience, very important, especially when dealing with people who maybe spoke Standard Terran, but not necessarily *'bleaker* Terran.

Not to mention dealing with people who had a whole 'nother language to think in, that no 'bleaker Darby knew could even begin to wrap their tongue around.

"Melon-tee?" he asked. "What's that?"

"Ah." Kestrel looked at Hestya. She laughed softly, and picked up her cup.

"*Melant'i*," he said. "*Melant'i*, as my colleague Zack would have it, is choosing which hat to wear in specific circumstances, given a very large possibility of hats. For instance, Hestya and I are colleagues. She works with me at the clinic, to ensure peace of mind and calmness in those who seek our aid.

"Hestya and I are also lovers," he continued. "However, when we are at the clinic, working, that part of our relative *melant'i's* is not. . .active. Do you see?"

"It is a concept that comes more easily, when one has learned the language," Hestya said. "Which—forgive me—I fear you will be required to do."

Darby looked at her.

"I don't know that I'm very good at learning languages, m—Hestya."

She smiled, and he felt, for the first time, her amusement, bright and sharp, like a new knife.

"Do you know?" she said; "I think you will prove to be very good at learning languages. Now."

She put her hands flat on the table, and looked at him very earnestly.

"You will be required to live at the Hall during the first phase of your instruction. It is our habit to assign an elder Healer to a novice, for both the safety of the House and the novice. Once you have mastered the core curriculum, you may choose to live outside of the House. When you are ready, Kestrel may commence his wooing, but you will tell him when you are ready, or if you are, indeed, interested in pursuing such a joint *melant'i*."

She gave him another one of her direct stares.

"I have overwhelmed your sensibilities," she murmured.

Darby laughed.

"You know that's not true," he said. "I want to learn—to learn how to use my gift for the best."

"Then we are in accord, we three friends. You have kin, Kestrel tells me, who depend upon your protection."

He frowned at her, then at Kestrel.

"Your sister and her children," he murmured.

"*Jewl?*" It was a shock, to think of Jewl needing *his* protection, and he was about put them right about who protected who, when he thought about Jewl huddled sick in her bed, and the boys alone when Farnch came home drunk and demanding his dinner.

Farnch. . .he coulda hurt the kids that night. Coulda hurt Jewl, too—killed her, maybe, if he'd managed to even half-rouse her. The reason it didn't get anywhere near that bad was *he'd* been there to deal with Farnch. Even had Kestrel by him to turn his brother's anger.

He looked at Hestya.

"Kestrel's right; I should talk to my sister. If Farnch gets mad. . ."

Or, he thought, *if he moves Vesti in over Jewl—sleet! That's just what he'll do, too; and Vesti ain't happy 'less somebody else ain't.*

"Peace." Hestya said. She extended a tiny hand and touched him for the first time, fingers curling 'round his wrist. He immediately felt calmer—more peaceful—and raised his eyes to hers.

"I thought you were s'posed to ask," he said.

She laughed, and removed her hand; leaving him grinning with a buoyancy that had little to do with peace.

"Kestrel, my friend, your felicity grows! Not only do you find for us a Terran Healer when none are said to exist, but he is quick, and observant—and lacks an appropriate sense of respect. He will, I think, do well."

"Shall we come with you, to your sister?" Kestrel asked. "She does not know either of us, and she will wish to satisfy herself that we mean you no harm."

"Sure," Darby said. "Let's do that now."

#

Miz Prestoro and Mister Warchiski were sitting on the stoop when him and Kestrel and Hestya came walking up the sidewalk, Kestrel carrying a sack full of the sweets they hadn't eaten, for the twins. He said.

"Brother's crew just brought 'im," Mister Warchiski said.

"Blood all over," Miz Prestoro added, and jerked her head up the street, opposite of where they'd come from. The sidewalk was wet.

"War 'n me, we hosed down the walk. Tinthy got 'em a blanket so he din't drip up the stairs."

Darby didn't wait; he flung himself up the stairs, two at a time, feeling Kestrel at his back. The door to their partment was half-open, he hit it with his shoulder without slowing down—

. . .and ran straight into Ornil, Farnch's third, who grabbed him and shook him, 'til Ron, Farnch's second, snarled at him.

"S'only the kid brother. You snow-blind?"

Ornil didn't let him go, but looked over his shoulder.

"*That* ain't no kid brother," he said, looking over Darby's shoulder

Riding the wash of angry surprise, Darby twisted, kicked Ornil hard in the knee, pushed him away, and threw himself hard against Ron, knocking him off balance before he could grab Kestrel.

"Leave 'im alone; he's a doctor!"

"He's a damn' Liaden, same's Farnch got shot up by!"

Ron pushed him; he staggered, caught himself, spun, and managed to get in front of Kestrel.

"You better go," Darby said over his shoulder.

"Indeed, I think I had better stay," Kestrel answered, and raised his voice. "I am a doctor. There is a wounded man in the house. Let me pass; I can help!"

"Let him through!" came another voice, from behind them. A hard voice, crackling with power. Ron and Ornil fell back, eyes wide, and—

"Let 'em through!" Jewl shouted from the kitchen. "My brother and the doctor, too!"

Darby felt a *push* go past his shoulder. Ornil and Ron went back another three steps, and he moved forward, toward the kitchen, feeling Kestrel, and something else, something like a wall of ice, walking behind him.

#

There was blood everywhere. Farnch was on the table, stripped to the waist. Vesti was pressing a towel soaked and dripping red against his shoulder. Gil was holding another against his side. Jewl had their kit out and open on the counter. Her sleeves were rolled up and she was bloody to the elbow. Darby saw her see him, and felt her relief; then she saw Kestrel and raised a hand, hope blazing like lightning.

"The bleeding won't stop."

"I understand," Kestrel said calmly, moving past Darby to Jewl's side. "Where are the children?"

"Down with Gran Delaros."

"Excellent," he said, reaching into his jacket for his little kit. "Now, tell me what has happened—he has been shot?"

"Damn' Liadens," Vesti spat.

"That is useful, thank you. If the pellets came from a Liaden gun, they will be of a different size than those in common use on the street here. Darby, my friend, please call the clinic. Ask them to send the taxi."

"No!" Vesti yelled. "Clinic'll call the Watch. *We was there*, you un-nerstand? We was with them taking a stand 'gainst the New Bosses! Watch'll arrest us all!"

Kestrel gave her a long stare.

"That may be," he said, cool-voiced. "But it is not the problem before us. Please move the compress, so that I may examine the wound."

Vesti snarled, grabbed the compress—and Darby felt a blast of freezing cold go past him.

Vesti froze in the act of throwing the bloody towel into Kestrel's face. Gil shifted—and he froze, too. Darby snaked past, out of the kitchen to the hall, where Hestya stood, face calm, eyes hard.

"You need help?" he asked, pausing at her side.

"I may, later," she answered, and he felt. . .something slip into the core of him, like she'd put a piece of candy into his hand. "Go, call the clinic; then return to help me watch these."

He nodded, and ran, past Ron and Ornil, who were sitting against the wall, eyes closed. Ornil was snoring.

* * *

"Well, I hope they'll be good to you, Darb," Jewl said, as she folded blankets into boxes. Her and the twins was moving, after all, to that new place closer to her work and the school.

Farnch—well, the Watch was gonna have him; they'd already taken up the rest of the crew. The New Bosses were gonna be holding trials, they said, for the ringleaders who had come out shooting against them. Farnch, and his crew, they hadn't quite been ringleaders. The New Bosses needed to make a Policy, word was, about what to do with the 'streeters who'd just kinda. . .gotten involved.

That wasn't Darby's problem, though. Not right now, it wasn't. He had his bag packed—not much stuff; clothes, books Dad'd given him. Pictures of Jewl and the twins.

"You come visit us, when they let you," his sister said, putting her hands on his shoulders, and kissing his cheek. Promise me, Darb."

"Promise," he said, and kissed her, too, then stepped out from under her hand, and walked down the hall, out the door, and down the stairs, where the taxi was waiting to take him to the Surebleak Healer Hall, and on to the rest of his life.

—end—

Friend of a Friend

Two young men, much of an age, but unalike in almost everything else, save having a good head for numbers, and a facility with the Sticks, walked down-Port toward the Emerald Casino.

They made a pretty picture—one tall and fair and lissome; the other supple and dark and golden-skinned. The fair lad wore a blue jacket, to set off his eyes. The dark one wore leather, and had a bag slung over his shoulder.

"So you'll be back in a Surebleak week?" the fair one asked, ending what had been a rather long pause between them.

His companion gave him an approving nod.

"That's pretty good, doing the conversions in your head on the fly."

"I've been practicing," Villy said. "I'll keep it up, too. By the time you're back, I'll be able to do a four-level conversion in my head!"

"Here's a bold assertion! Will books be all of your lovers, until I am returned to your arms?"

Villy considered him out of suspicious blue eyes.

"*That* sounds like a play-quote," he said.

"Discovered!"

Quin gave a small, on-the-stride bow of acknowledgment—for which he would have been severely reprimanded had he been observed by his protocol teacher—or, twelve times worse!—his grandmother.

"It is a play-quote, yes. If you like, I'll find a tape and we may watch it together."

"Would I? Like it, I mean."

That was a serious question, and Quin gave it the consideration it deserved.

"You might well. It's a classic *melant'i* play, and I had to study it, and write papers on it, and view several productions, from the first recorded to the most modern, which is why I have the phrase so apt, you see. But—yes, I think you might find it useful, and interesting, too. Especially the sword fight."

"Sword fight?"

"The most diverting thing imaginable, and quite harrowing, despite you know it's all mummery."

"OK, then, I'm provisionally interested. If I get bored, though, I'll make you speed through to the sword fight."

"Fair enough."

The casino was in sight; they would part in another few minutes. Villy was bound for the Sticks table and his shift as dealer. Quin was for Korval's yard, *Galandasti*, and Pilot Tess Lucien, who was to sit his second, who had undoubtedly arrived early, and would therefore believe that he was late. . .

"What will you do," he asked, "while I am away?"

Villy looked arch.

"Jealous, honey? I'll keep busy, don't you worry. And books won't be half of it."

Quin laughed, Villy grinned, and stepped close to drop a kiss on Quin's cheek.

"You fly safe now, handsome," he said, huskily, and slipped away to join a group of the casino's morning workers, calling out to Cassie to wait for him.

Quin shook his head, his cheek burning where Villy's lips had brushed. For Liadens, such a salutation was given between kin, or lifemates, or—perhaps—long-time lovers.

For Villy, a kiss on the cheek denoted casual affection. Or, as Villy himself had it, "I kiss all my friends."

Yes, well. Local custom. It was Quin's part to step away from the custom—and Villy, too—if he was offended.

Which, truth told, he was not.

Surely, his grandmother was correct when she deplored the state of his *melant'i*.

His father had nothing to say regarding Quin's friendship with the best Sticks dealer the Emerald employed. In fact, he and Villy had met over the Sticks table, and the relationship had been firmly fixed before Quin discovered that Villy was also one of the company of *hetaerana* attached to Ms. Audrey's house of delights.

Quin had been tutored in the protocols of pleasure, though circumstances had not granted him much opportunity to refine his knowledge. From observation, however, it would seem that Terrans and Liadens approached bed-sport on vastly different trajectories, and merely being among the number of Villy's *friends* meant receiving casual kisses on the street. A Liaden *hetaera* would blush to presume so far on the *melant'i* of even a frequent partner-in-joy.

And, again. . .local custom

"We will all need to be scouts, if we mean to settle here," Quin had said to Grandfather Luken, who had only laughed.

"But we *have* settled here, boy-dear! Never fear that your grandmother will find us a way to a new Code. In the meanwhile, your father is not *quite* an idiot, as you know, nor are his fellow Bosses. They teach and learn in equal measure. What remains for us is to be slow to take offense, and to cultivate the *melant'i* of a little child."

Children—*little* children—were understood to stand within the *melant'i* of their clan. Their own *melant'i* was. . .flexible and open, and very specifically did not pursue Balance. It was tradition, to give a child upon their twelfth Name Day a Small Debt Book, in which entries were made by the child, and reviewed with a clan elder. On the fourteenth Name Day, a private Debt Book was given, and it was considered at that point that the child was competent to take up the keeping of their own *melant'i*, and Balances.

On consideration, Quin thought that Luken might have the right of it.

He also thought that most of the Liadens who had followed Korval to Surebleak were not. . .capable of accepting the *melant'i* of a little child. Most especially if it also meant tolerating insults from Terrans.

It really was too bad that Father hadn't chosen a civilized world to subjugate to Korval's purpose.

Quin threaded his way through the ships sleeping in Korval's Yard. There, just ahead, was *Galandasti*, and, as he had feared, there also was Pilot Lucien, her long self disposed down half-a-dozen gantry steps, from the tread where she leaned her elbows, to the stair where her boots rested.

"Well, there you are! I was starting to wonder if you wanted to fly today, after all."

He felt his ears warm, and his temper rise—which was nonsense; hadn't he known how it would be? The good pilot was always early; he, by extension, was always late.

"I think we can make up the time," he said evenly, for, in addition to being annoying, Pilot Lucien was a master pilot, in charge of observing him, and of registering his flight time with the Guild.

"I have the package. If you will do me the honor of ascending and waking the board, I will do the walkaround."

Pilot Lucien's hair fell in jagged points to her jawbone, the ends were dyed silver and purple; the rest was dull black. The silver and purple distracted as she tipped her head, and looked at him through narrowed eyes.

"Did the walkaround while I was waiting," she said.

Quin's temper flared again. Really, did she think he was a fool?

He took a breath and calmed himself. Of course, it was a test. This whole flight would be a test. There would doubtless, therefore, be many instances in which his temper was tried.

Best, then, to practice patience.

He produced a smile for the pilot.

"Thank you. I am accustomed to doing a walkaround myself; it soothes me and prepares my mind for the lift. I doubt that the ship will take harm from having the eyes of two pilots upon it."

She shrugged and came to her feet.

"Suit yourself," she said shortly, and went up the gantry, her boots clanging on each stair.

Teeth grit, Quin ducked under the gantry to begin the Pilot's Pre-Lift Visual Inspection, precisely as outlined in the handbook.

* * *

"Busy night?" Cassie asked him three days later, when they were again on the early shift together.

Villy liked Cassie. She didn't mind about his other job, like some of the crew did; just treated it like. . .well. . .another job.

"Not busy at all," he said ruefully, "so I got the idea to study, and *that* turned into *late*."

"Didn't you remember you had the early shift here?"

"I remembered, all right! I can't tell you how many times I said to myself, *Villim, cut it off, you gotta work early tomorrow*! Didn't do a bit of good!"

Cassie laughed.

"What're you studying that's so absorbing?"

"Communication," Villy said, oversimplifying wildly. "We're getting a lot of new clients who ain't—aren't—from Surebleak, just like we get here at the casino. I'm studying up on what's comfortable, and what's not, and bows—that's useful here, too. . ."

Cassie's smile had faded into something serious-looking.

"That's pretty smart," she said, which it was, and Villy would've felt proud of thinking of it, but he hadn't—not exactly. He'd only said out something that he'd been thinking, about not feeling like he was offering everything he could to the new custom, because he didn't know the rules. He didn't have any idea beyond his own frustration, really; it'd been Quin who identified the problem and figured out a way to maybe deal with it.

"Do you think you could lend me the tapes, when you're done with them?" Cassie asked, waving her card at the clock. "Or maybe we could study together? I'd really like to get a handle on them bows. For starters."

Well, no, he couldn't lend the tapes. For one thing, they weren't tapes; they were lessons Quin had archived from his school. He'd been a tutor, so he'd been able to give Villy a passcode to access the basic lessons. Supplemental data and tests and stuff were only available to Quin's code.

Anyway, nothing he could share with Cassie.

He stepped up and waved his badge. The clock beeped acceptance, and he stepped over to where Cassie was waiting for him.

"You know what we should do?" he said brightly.

"What's that?" Cassie said, and he appreciated it that she didn't smirk or wink or make a joke.

Villy paused, briefly having no idea what he was going to say, then heard himself speak up.

"We oughta ask Beny to organize a class. Then we could all learn together, and. . ."

He stopped because Cassie was staring at him.

"What?"

"That's brilliant. Villy, that's *brilliant*!"

"Well, it's not. I mean, I was so focused on how to do better at my other job, I didn't even think about here, until you asked me what I was studying. Then it all sort of clicked."

He gave her a smile. It was one of his professional smiles: two parts shy and one part mischief, and she smiled back, the muscles in her face and shoulders relaxing.

There, he thought, pleased; that's better.

"I'll talk to Beny on my first break," he offered. Cassie shook her head.

"I'm covering for Joon this morning, upstairs. I'll be seeing him right off and I'll mention your idea to him."

"It's your idea as much as it's mine!" he said, but Cassie only smiled and waggled her fingers at him in good-bye, turning toward the stairs.

Villy sighed, and headed for the Sticks table.

#

The casino was bustling but not overcrowded, which was usual for the morning shift. Most of the players were late-nighters, still at the tables, with a smattering of the regulars who stopped in on their way to work to drop a coin in one of the machines, or roll a round of dice. Pretty soon, they'd get the night-workers comin' in, ready maybe for some longer play at the wheel, or the card tables.

Or the Sticks.

All in all, Villy kept tolerably busy until it was time for his mid-morning break. Sonit came to relieve him as the last players left the table, both of them considerably lighter in the pocketbook. Villy's knees were shaking some, and his forehead was damp. The House had won, fair. The House nearly always won, though Boss Conrad, who owned the Emerald, said the Sticks were an honest game of skill, more like cards than like dicing—or the wheel. The House was *expected* to win against most comers 'cause the Sticks dealer was an experienced and skilled player.

This time, though. . .The players had insisted on playing three-way, with the House taking a full part. Usually, Villy only played single players. Playing against two—well, he'd done it before, but it was uncommon *and* nerve-wracking.

He'd demonstrated his skill, though, and the House'd won, though he'd gotten a bad jolt when he'd thought the orange stick was gonna roll off the table. . .

"Everything OK?" Sonit asked.

"Yeah. Just finished up a three-way is all."

Sonit whistled.

"Better you'n me. Gwon and getcher coffee. I'll stand here an' just sorta glare and scare 'em all away."

That wasn't a joke. Sonit wasn't anything more than a good enough Sticks dealer, and not much of a player, but he *was* big and intimidating, and his frown was almost a physical shove in the chest. A player had to have a death-wish to approach the Sticks table while Sonit was presiding.

"I'll be back soon," Villy said.

Sonit grinned broadly, which made him look even more savage than his frown. Villy shook his head, and held up his hands.

"I'm going," he said. "Don't hurt me."

"Like I could lay a hand on you," Sonit said, his grin softening into a really attractive smile. "Git."

Villy got.

#

He was at his usual table in the break room, overlooking the floor, coffee and a cookie to keep him comfortable. He enjoyed looking down on the playing floor, seeing all the stations laid out like a map, and the players moving between them like leaves ahead of a snow wind. Lately, he'd taken to studying different styles of walking, and thinking about what each style told about the walker, or their culture. He'd shown Quin the game, one day when he was working the casino backroom, and they'd met for lunch.

Quin had been interested—and good, too, which wasn't a surprise. Quin had fast eyes and if he wasn't the sharpest knife in the drawer, he'd do 'til something fatal came along.

Villy took a bite out of his cookie and washed it down with hot coffee.

The locals, they kinda scuffed along the floor—that was from having to walk on ice and snow most of the time. You didn't want to slip and fall, so you sorta half-skated along. Liadens walked tall and broad, for all they was skinny and short—world-bound Liadens, anyhow. Off-world Terrans walked with knees slightly bent, and hands away from their body, like they might have to grab something fast to keep from falling, which made sense, 'cause most of the off-world Terrans were spacers. And it was kind of funny, 'til you thought about it, that the space-faring Liadens—the pilots and the crewfolk—they walked like the Terrans: soft in the knees and ready to snatch a grab-bar.

Scouts now, they walked soft, and sort of swayed, like every muscle was loose. Their heads hardly moved, despite which, they saw *every*thing. Quin said it was because Scouts had quick eyes, and quicker ears.

Mercs—Terran *or* Liaden—marched tall, looking left-then-right, footsteps falling firm enough that when a group of them went through the casino, you could feel 'em hit, even 'way up in control.

Security—well, there was Security now in the shapes of Big Haz and Tolly. Haz, she walked like a Scout, quiet and loose, and eyes moving. Tolly. . .Tolly was a puzzle. Sometimes, he walked Surebleak, sometimes he walked spacer. Other times—just for a step or two, and you had to be watching sharp to catch it—*sometimes* he walked like a hunter cat, muscles oiled and chin up, like he was scenting lunch nearby.

Right now, he was pure 'bleaker, leaning on the bar and talking with Herb. Haz stood tall beside him and a little behind, like she always did, alert to the room, and just as relaxed as if she had eyes in the back of her. . .

"Hey, Villy."

A chair scraped as Beny, the day-side crew boss, slid in across the table.

"Hey," Villy said. "Cassie talk to you?"

"'S'why I'm here. That's a good idea you had about the seminar. We all got the basic training when we were hired on, but you're right; it's time to go to the next level. We don't just got spacers and locals; we got people who expect the comforts of home. So, anyhow, I just wanted to tell you—I ran it by Mr. Conrad, and he's gonna hire us a *protocol master*—prolly be a Scout, he said—and we'll have lessons in how to be a little easier on Liaden eyes. Mr. Conrad, he was firm that he didn't want us to cross over into looking too Liaden for our core clientele, but we still got room to bend. It was smart of you to notice."

"I didn't know I'd noticed 'til I was talking with Cassie," Villy said, dunking his cookie in his coffee.

"Right, right. She said that, too. Now, here, I know your break's just about over, so I'll get done and leave you to finish up."

Beny reached into his vest pocket and pulled out an envelope. He put it on the table, and pushed it toward Villy.

"What's that?"

"Don't you read the sign by the clock? Anybody comes up with an idea about how to make the casino run better, or increase profit, gets a reward if Mr. Conrad accepts the idea. Mr. Conrad accepted the idea, and you get fifty cash. Pretty good, huh?"

Fifty cash was a nice bit of money, but—

"I didn't earn that."

"Says so on the wall. Gwon and read it when you punch back in. Which you better start thinking about." Beny got up, leaving the envelope behind him.

"Good thinkin', Villy," he said, and left.

Alone, Villy finished his cookie and coffee while staring at the envelope.

Fifty cash for saying they ought to learn how to bow better? That was like. . .free money.

On the other hand, he thought, pushing back his chair and coming to his feet, there wasn't anything wrong with free money.

Was there?

He sighed sharply, grabbed the envelope and shoved it into an inner pocket of his vest.

#

It was coming up on shift-change, and Villy was looking forward to going home and having a nap before he had to get ready for his other job. He'd just finished watching Margit Pince lose her day-pay on a solo Sticks fall. Once a week, she lost a day's pay at his table, and he really wished she wouldn't. Couldn't talk her out of it, though; not his job. His job was to suppose she could afford the loss, and to witness the play to be sure it was fairly done. He wished she'd give up the Sticks, but there wasn't any sign she was going to, anytime soon. She considered them a challenge, and she was determined to beat them—which she wouldn't, anytime soon, in Villy's professional judgment. Unfortunately, she'd gotten—*a little*—better, which only encouraged her to continue to play.

Honestly, Margit was one of the few downsides of the casino job. His gran used to say that grown-ups chose for themselfs, and Margit was a grown-up. So. He took a deep breath and settled himself. Not his problem; he'd done his job.

There not being anybody looking to step up and take Margit's place at the table, Villy started to straighten the drawer, so the dealer next-shift could just open right up. He collected the tokens into their bag, and updated the tally sheet; lined the wrapped and sealed bundles up: twenty-fours all together at the top, thirty-sixes beneath; eighteen stick bundles tucked in their own compartment down the length of the drawer.

The bigger bundles were standard offers at Liaden casinos. The bundle of eighteen—called Quick Sticks—was a Surebleak variation, offered only at the Emerald casino, and approved by no less a gamester than Pat Rin yos'Phelium.

Pat Rin yos'Phelium, that was Boss Conrad's real, Liaden name. Not many people knew that, though it was right there to be figured out, by those who paid attention.

Most people, though, they didn't pay attention, though it ought've been plain that, if Boss Conrad and the Road Boss were brothers, and the Road Boss didn't make no secret of his name being Val Con yos'Phelium, that Boss Conrad's real name ought at least to have *yos'Phelium* in it somewhere.

Even though it wasn't true that the bosses were brothers—he'd asked Quin, who'd said they were cousins, though it was true that Quin's father—that being Pat Rin—was the older of the two.

"Likely they decided it was simpler for those not familiar with Liaden Lines to understand them as brothers, and such a simplification did no damage to their *melant'i*."

Quin'd been laying on his side on Villy's bed, his head propped on his hand. He'd paused for a second, staring hard at nothing, which meant he was weighing something in his mind.

"There was the matter of the two Rings, also. . ." he said, quiet, like he was talking to himself before he said, louder and firmer, "Yes, I think they decided for simplicity."

He'd smiled at Villy.

"After all, I agreed to have had a younger brother, for much the same reasons. It does me no harm to honor the memory of a boy who had placed himself under my father's protection. Had he survived, we might well have been declared foster-brothers. That being so, why should I not agree with what is already widely known?"

That bidness—about Quin's younger brother—that was about Jonni, who'd been a kid in Boss Conrad's house, and gotten in the middle of a firefight. The story'd gone out on the street that Jonni'd been the Boss' own son, which Villy'd known wasn't true. Jonni's ma'd worked for Ms. Audrey. She never did say who was his father; might've been she hadn't know. Or that she had, and thought her boy'd be better off without 'im.

Villy'd tried to splain that, once, to somebody who knew the street story, and who didn't care to believe anything else. That had kinda cured him of ever trying to splain it again.

Well, no wonder the bosses just accepted what the street said; they might as well save their breath for—

Something moved in the corner of his eye. He looked up from the drawer, smiling slightly and impersonally at the Liaden woman approaching the table. She wasn't wearing leather, but she walked like a spacer, with some merc mixed in.

"Buy a bundle, ma'am? We have Solcintran Sticks in packets of twenty-four and thirty-six. Or, if you're pressed for time, we also offer the local eighteen-stick variation."

"Thank you," she said.

She smiled at him. Some of the world-bound Liadens were trying to learn to smile at Terrans, having heard that Terrans liked to be smiled at. Their efforts usually ran from faintly unsettling to painful.

This was the first smile Villy'd gotten from a Liaden that was outright terrifying.

He swallowed and bowed his head, like he was welcoming her, but it was really to hide his face. His foot twitched toward the panic switch on the floor under the table, but he stopped it just short of connecting.

"I believe," the Liaden said, "that you are a companion to Quin yos'Phelium, as I am myself. I wonder if you might tell me his direction."

That was off; his mouth tasted sour, that's how *off* it was. Sure, him and Quinn were friends, but there wasn't no reason for this stranger to know, or care about, once she'd come to know it. Quin's father *owned* the Emerald, didn't he? And if she was one of Quin's friends, wouldn't she *know* that?

He took a breath, thought about the panic switch again, and decided it was better not to make a fuss. That being so, he got his professional smile into place and looked up to meet her eyes.

"I can't talk about that here," he said. "My *melant'i's* Sticks dealer, right now."

She blinked—he'd surprised her—and inclined her head.

"Of course," she said, polite enough; "I understand. Good-day to you."

She turned and walked away, giving off that mixed vibe of merc and spacer.

Villy let out the breath he'd been holding, and closed his eyes.

When he opened them again, Sara was on his side of the table, tally-sheet in hand.

"Time to go home, hon!" she said cheerfully.

He gave her a grin, though it felt a little uncertain on his mouth.

"Already? I was having so much fun, I thought I'd do a double."

"Nope, nope. My turn to have some fun. You've had enough."

"Right, then," Villy said. He patted her arm, and scooted out from behind the table.

Going across the floor to the stairs, he kept an eye out for the woman who'd wanted Quin's *direction*. He didn't see her, which might've meant she'd left—or maybe she'd smartened up and asked one of the Security Team to take her to the Boss.

Either way, it wasn't none of his bidness. He just hoped he'd never see her again.

* * *

Villy woke up from his nap in plenty of time to eat dinner and get ready for his regular date with Bradish Faw.

Bradish was one of his favorite dates, and not just because he brought a platter of pastries every week to share out among the whole crew, and a special treat, tied up in colored cellophane with a big bow, for Villy himself. No, he liked Bradish because the baker was genuinely kind, and because no date was exactly the same as all the others. Sometimes, Bradish would bring a book and ask Villy to read to him, sometimes he'd bring a music tape, sometimes he would bring a toy or something special he wanted—or wanted Villy—to wear.

Tonight, Bradish hugged him, then held him at arm's length, looking him up and down.

"You been worryin'?" he asked severely.

"Studying," Villy answered with a smile. "Does it show?"

"I saw it, din't I? Nothin' wrong with studyin', but you don't wanna lose your looks over it."

He released Villy and looked around the room, his eye lighting on the low table with the toys laid out, and the oil on its warming tile.

"Oil nice and warm?" he asked.

"Ought to be. I'll check it while you make yourself comfy."

"No, you get comfy, and I'll check it. I ain't give you a massage in too long."

Dates went the way the client said they did, within limits set out in the House Rules—that was a House Rule, too. Villy slipped his robe off, stretched out on his stomach, and put his head down on his crossed arms. He heard the sound of Bradish getting undressed, and raised his head again.

"Want me to help you with that, honey?" he asked, husky and suggestive.

"You just stay right there," Bradish told him, "where I can 'preciate the view."

There was some more rustling, then a gentle clink which was probably the oil bottle being lifted off the tile. The bed gave when Bradish knelt beside him, and Villy shivered when warm, knowing hands stroked his back and sides.

"Beautiful," Bradish said, moving his hands away. "Let's get you relaxed."

The hands were back, oiled this time, strong fingers finding the knots in his shoulders and the tight places along his spine and patiently smoothing them away.

Villy sighed—and sighed again, as his muscles loosened. Over his head, his date laughed softly.

"You melt like butter on a griddle," he murmured, his breath warm in Villy's ear. He shivered obligingly, and Bradish returned to the massage.

When he was thoroughly oiled, utterly melted, and almost half-asleep, Bradish leaned over him, murmuring in his ear. Villy lifted his head; Bradish gently pushed it back down onto his arms.

"You just stay like you are. I'll take care of everything," he whispered.

#

Some while later, Bradish having left for home, the sheets changed and hygiene observed, Villy went downstairs. Bidness'd been light the last few days. Even though he was still feeling languorous and drifty, he really ought to take another date tonight, if there was anybody waiting in the parlor for company. In the event that there was, he was wearing fluid dark pants, and a see-through white shirt. The new rug in the downstairs hall felt nice under his bare toes as he headed for the parlor.

"Hey, Villy," Jade said as he paused by the desk beside the parlor door. Jade was on reception tonight, keeping track of requests, who went upstairs with who, and how long they were logged for.

"Hey, sweetie," he said, smiling at her. "Anybody lonely in the parlor?"

"Nothing to worry you, if there are. You been reserved. Paid cash upfront, too, for a whole two hours."

Villy blinked. Two hours was pretty rich. Then he realized that it had to be one of his pilots, back on-port and looking for company. He didn't wince, though vigorous pilot exercise wasn't quite what he wanted after Bradish's treatment. But, two hours paid up full wasn't something he could afford to pitch aside just because he wasn't feeling athletic.

"I'll just get a cup of coffee first," he said to Jade. "What his name, my date?"

Jade shook her head.

"The lady said her name was Desa ven'Zel. Liaden—well, with that name, what else?—and she asked for you, specific."

Villy felt a cold breath of air down the back of his thin shirt. Suddenly, he was a lot more awake.

"Lemme see the screen," he said, and Jade obligingly spun it around to him.

There were four clients in the parlor. Three streeters were talking with Nan, Vera, and Si, for values of talking that involved lap-cuddles and nuzzling. The fourth client sat in the chair nearest the fireplace, hands folded on her knee, pensive gaze directed to the hearth stone.

Villy spun the screen back to Jade, wide awake now.

"Who's bouncing?" he asked.

"Patsy."

"Buzz her and ask her to meet me at the coffeepot."

"You're not taking the date?"

Villy shook his head, emphatically.

Jade didn't frown, but she did say, "I need something to put in the log."

"Not safe," Villy said, which wasn't something you put down in the log lightly. *Not safe*, meant that Ms. Audrey would never open to this particular client again.

"I'll buzz Patsy," Jade said. "Go get your coffee, Villy; you look green."

#

". . .at the casino. She said she was a friend of Quin's, like I was, and wanted me to tell her where to find him. I—something felt off, is all, an' I brushed her off, told her my *melant'i* didn't let me talk right then."

"Took that, did she?" Patsy asked. She was leaning against the wall by the buffet, watching him drink his coffee.

Villy nodded.

"Took it. Shift went over 'bout then. I looked out for her on the floor when I left. Didn't see her and figured somebody smarter'n me'd sent her up to the Boss."

Patsy nodded.

"Shoulda been the way it went, if she was after where was Quin," she said in her deep, quiet voice. "Her comin' here, after *you*, again—either she *didn't* get her answer from the Boss, or she *did*, and took a fancy to you, separate from that bidness."

Villy's stomach cramped. He held his coffee cup in icy hands and looked up at Patsy.

"I don't want to talk to her," he said. "She scares me."

She eyed him.

"Considering the people I've seen who *don't* scare you, that's pretty tellin'. Quiet a minute, now; I gotta think this out."

Patsy stared up into the corner of the room. Villy felt his stomach sink. Nothing good could come outta Patsy's thinking about this. Dammit, there wasn't anything to think *about!* It was open and shut; he had the right to refuse any client he considered was dangerous—that was in the Rules a couple times, put down in different ways.

"Where *is* Quin?" Patsy asked abruptly.

"Offworld making a delivery," Villy told her, and put his cup down, still half-full of coffee. Patsy had thought something out and he was pretty sure he wasn't going to like whatever she'd decided on.

"So," she said pensively, "we got this Liaden woman asking the Sticks dealer does he know where's the Boss' son? Even if she's a friend, she still might know anything more particular about where he is, past *Surebleak*. Still an' all, why ask the Sticks dealer? Why *not* ask the Boss—or McFarland, if the Boss was too busy to talk?"

Villy didn't answer; the questions weren't for him; they were to help Patsy fix her reasoning. She was working her way up to something, and he didn't like the direction she was tending toward.

"Patsy, *I don't wanna* talk to her."

Her eyes focused on him; she gave him a smile and patted his shoulder.

"I know you don't, sweetie. Stick here just another sec. I gotta check something with Jade."

She left, walking fast. Villy considered going up to his room, but Patsy was perfectly capable of getting Ms. Audrey to order him to come out and do what he was told.

He sighed, looked at the coffee cup he'd put down—and didn't pick it up again. Which was a good thing, because here came Patsy back again, her face firm and professional.

"OK," she said briskly. "Your date's starting to get impatient."

"I said I didn't want the date," Villy said, as patient as he could. "Jade can tell her that, and give the deposit back."

"Well, she might've done that," Patsy said, as one being fair, "'cept I butted in and told her you'd be right down." She held up a hand to stop him squawking, so he just shook his head.

"Look, this—whatever *this* is—bears on the Boss' household. She might *be* a friend—though McFarland didn't know anything 'bout nobody looking for Quin today. From t'other side, she might *not* be a friend, which fits with the pieces we got. Either side, it's Boss Conrad's to solve. McFarland'll be here inside ten minutes. All you hafta do is keep her in the parlor 'til he gets here and takes her in hand."

"Give her money back and set her out on the street. Cheever can take 'er up there," Villy said, knowing it wasn't going to go that way. Patsy's mind was made up, and, well, sleet—what was ten minutes? He could talk that long in his sleep.

"No, now, you're not thinkin'. We don't want to put ourselfs in the way of Balance, now, do we? Because we're nice, sensible people who don't wanna get shot today, or to get put on a list to get shot five years down the road when we're least expecting it, because we interfered where we shouldn't've. So, if this lady wants Quin, and Quin ain't here, then the very best thing we can do is get her into the hands of Quin's dad—and Quin's dad's 'hand—who'll know zackly what to do with her, and how to do it."

Put that way—well, he was thinking now, if he hadn't been, before. He didn't believe for a minute that Desa ven'Zel was any friend of Quin's. That didn't mean they didn't know each other, anyhow, and maybe *did* have bidness—Liaden bidness—to do together. Either way, Patsy was right; they didn't want to tangle themselves—and maybe the whole of Ms. Audrey's house, too—in any Liaden Balances.

Villy sighed, quietly. He knew what Patsy wanted him to do, and if it had been anyone else—well, sleet, it was what he *did do*, a lot of the time, if somebody was upset, or rambunctious—*get Villy*, that's what they said, and he'd come and get 'em all settled down. That was all this was, really, soothe the lady's impatience, and keep her busy talking 'til Cheever came and took her in hand.

"All right. But I don't want her in my room."

Patsy smiled at him.

"You don't worry about that; she's not going anywhere outside that parlor. Just all you gotta do is talk to her 'til McFarland gets here," she said soothingly. "I'll be watching the whole time. If she tries to hurt you, I'm there. Promise."

"Even if it means she puts you down on her list?"

"Sweetie, you're more important to me than any Liaden's shit list. I started living on borrowed time a year or two before you was borned."

He took a breath. *All you gotta do is talk to her*, he told himself. *Give 'er an on-the-house drink and ask after what she likes and how she likes it. Keep her from killing Jade*—that was an uncomfortable thought, but he didn't doubt the aptness of it. He looked at Patsy.

"Time for Jade's coffee break, maybe," he said.

Patsy narrowed her eyes.

"I think you're right," she said, with hardly a pause to think on it. "I'll relieve her while you go in to see your date."

"Right," Villy said.

He breathed in, and breathed out, which he pretended calmed his stomach, and headed for the parlor, stride loose and face languid.

#

"I have been waiting for you," she said, rising as he came into the room.

Villy looked around the room; the three couples had apparently moved upstairs, and he was alone in the parlor with the Liaden woman— Desa ven'Zel—who was at least not smiling. Her face wasn't really doing much of anything; it was like she'd painted it over with clear glue. If her greeting was a complaint, you couldn't read it in her expression, or in her eyes.

Villy gave a little smile of his own.

"I didn't know you were waiting, honey," he said, carefully avoiding anything that sounded like an apology. "I'd've been down sooner, if I had."

"I made an appointment," she said. "The person at the desk was to have told you."

"Well, but my last date went over," Villy said, improvising; "and I didn't check my messages right away, after I was alone." He gave her another smile, purely professional, and made a show of looking her over and liking what he saw.

"There's no reason for us to fight; I'm here now, and we can get to know each other." He moved over to the refreshments table, wondering how many minutes he'd used up outta Patsy's ten. His nerves said it'd been a year since he'd come into the parlor, but his head was arguing for under two minutes.

"What would you like to drink?" he asked over his shoulder.

"I would like nothing to drink," she said sternly. "I desire to go to your rooms. There are. . ." She hesitated, and he turned to look at her, which was a mistake, because it encouraged her to smile.

"There are. . .*very special things* that I wish you to do for me."

Villy managed to suppress his shudder, and smiled back.

"I'm looking forward to that," he said. "But the first thing we gotta do is sit down and talk a little bit about the House Rules. The very first House Rule is that we have to talk about 'em with all our new dates, so there's no misunderstandings or. . .*unwanted* surprises. This is a house of pleasure," he said, warming slightly to his topic; "we don't want any. . .mistakes."

The smile had slipped off of her mouth, leaving it hard and straight. He thought he saw impatience in the set of her face, but she bowed her head nice enough.

"Indeed, all should be informed of the House Rules," she murmured. "Mistakes are very costly, as I'm sure your Ms. Audrey would agree." She raised her chin. "For the drink, is there wine?"

"Sure there is," he said heartily, knowing that what he had on offer wasn't anything close to the beverage she'd expect. "I've got lorinberry wine, dandyweed wine, and soran wine right here, all nice and cold."

She considered him out of narrowed eyes.

"Soran wine is sweet?" she asked finally.

"Sweet as love," he assured her.

"I will have that."

"Good choice. Why don't you take a seat and get comfy while I pour for us?"

#

He'd hoped she'd go back to the single chair she'd been sitting in, absent his specific invitation to get comfy on one of the couches. The hope was dashed when he turned, glasses in hand, to find her curled into the corner of the softest, and least easily escaped couch Ms. Audrey owned.

She smiled, and patted the cushion beside her.

He crossed the room, frantically wondering how long it had been *now*, handed her a glass and settled in beside her.

She lifted her glass, by which he knew she meant to offer a toast. He lifted his glass in imitation.

"To successful endeavors," she said, which sounded a little strange for a toast from a client to a host in a whorehouse. Villy raised his glass in answer.

"Successful endeavors," he murmured, and sipped.

The wine was icy, and so sweet the inside of his mouth puckered for a moment. Even Desa ven'Zel seemed momentarily speechless.

Villy took a breath.

"A question," his so-called date said.

"Sure."

"Is this time that we linger over the rules deducted from the amount I placed upon deposit?"

Worried about her money, was she? Villy guessed he didn't blame her. He gave her a reassuring smile and reached over to pat her knee, which was the last thing he wanted to do, but, under other circumstances, was the thing *he would have done*. It was like patting a rock, except that a rock couldn't narrow its eyes. And she wanted him to do *very special things* to her? When snowballs got up and danced a jig, she did.

He sipped his wine and got his hand back without making it seem like he couldn't let go of her soon enough; and smiled again.

"The talk and the drink's on the house," he told her, which was true for every new client. "The clock won't start ticking on that deposit until we close the door on our bedroom."

"That is well," she said, and leaned forward to put a hand on his thigh.

That was a surprise, and what was more of a surprise was that she kept it there. Her fingers were cold through the thin pants, and her grip was hard and impersonal. Away in another part of the house, he could just make out voices. The doorman was sending visitors down to the overflow parlor. That meant Ms. Audrey knew what was going on, and approved it. The House was making sure him and his date weren't disturbed.

"So," she said, and her fingers tightened until it *hurt*. He drew a sharp breath, looked into her eyes, and gasped again at her smile.

"Tell me the rules, Villy Butler."

She leaned back into her corner then, taking her hand with her. He'd had a bruise for sure, and—

Where the *sleet* was Cheever McFarland? Villy thought, in a sudden spike of raw terror.

He took a breath and pushed it out of his head, pushed *all of it* out of his head. For the length of the date, he concentrated on the date. He pretended—only it wasn't pretend, not zackly—that the date was the most important thing in his life. The *only* thing in his life. That was the way it worked. Let yourself get distracted and the date noticed. Even if they didn't know *what* they'd noticed, they wouldn't ask for Villy again. . .

"The Rules," he said, smiling into her eyes. "Since you want me to do *really special things*, let's talk about those Rules."

He had a sip of his wine, still holding her eyes with his, though he didn't want anything else, except to look away.

"There's no cutting, no flogging, no carving, no burning—nothing that draws blood, or does harm, is what I'm saying. There's no choking, no crushing, and nothing that breaks bones.

"Bondage, spanking, rough play—all allowed under the Rules; rough as you like it, without crossing the lines we just talked about.

"Before we go to a room, host and guest each picks a quit-word. That's everybody, no matter what. Even if all you wanna do is take a nap together."

He smiled at her then, in such a way as to suggest that a nap was at the bottom of a long list of activities he wanted to share with her.

"The quit-word—if you say yours or I say mine, that's the signal for everything to *stop*. The person who used their word tells out what happened to make them wanna quit, and the session's done."

"Does the patron receive a refund for time unused?" his date asked him. Woman was tight with her money.

"Ms. Audrey decides," he said.

She nodded, and leaned over, supple as a snake.

"I am told that Terrans. . .like this," she said, holding his eyes with hers. "Is it so?"

She stroked the back of her fingers very lightly down the side of his face. Villy shuddered, he couldn't help it. He hoped she'd think it was desire, and managed not to pull away, and *where* was McFarland?

Desa ven'Zel smiled, and gripped him by the chin, fingers tightening.

"The Rules. . ." he whispered, and he thought for a moment that she was going to *laugh*, and if she did, the sound of it would kill him outright.

"The Rules," she murmured, instead, her fingers holding his chin in a grip that was just next to painful. "The House seeks to maximize its profit, and minimize its expense. Therefore, it limits accidents, which are, as we have agreed, expensive."

She released his chin, trailing her fingers down his throat and his chest, where the shirt was open, and rested her palm flat on his abdomen.

"You are very pretty," she said, which he'd heard before. But he'd never heard it said like it was an insult. "Do you bring the House much profit?"

"Sweetie. . ." He wanted her hand *off* of him, dammit; he wanted out of here; he wanted a shower—two showers!

"Sweetie," he said again, hearing his voice wobble; "that ain't polite to ask."

"Is it not?"

Her eyebrows rose, but she didn't take her hand away.

"I will remember. Are there more Rules, or may we go to your room, now?"

There were more Rules, all right, including that he could tell the bouncer he considered a client unsafe, and *refuse the date*. Better not tell her that one, though. Thundering blizzards, how did Quin *know* this woman?

"One more," he said, and dragged up what he hoped she'd take for the smile of a man just managing to keep his arousal in check, rather than a man who was scared outta his mind.

"You wanna take that hand back, before something. . .goes off."

The look she gave him might've melted lead, but she took her hand away.

"Since you're a lady who's careful with her money, I gotta tell you this—sometimes a visit'll go a little over-time, and if it does, the House expects to be paid for the extra time. I try to make sure that we'll wind up on time, but sometimes, everything's clicking along, and neither one wants to stop while it's good. If you *do* wanna stop at the end of your reserved time, we'll tell the desk before we go up. They'll send somebody to open the door, in case we don't hear the timer."

"I understand. Come."

She stood, putting her cup on the side table as she did.

"Come?" He looked up at her. "There's more Rules."

"You will relate them later, or you will instruct me if I have inadvertently offended the House."

Damn. He *didn't* want her in his room. He *didn't* want to be alone with her any more. He wanted—

He raised his hand.

"You wanted me to do special things, you said. Can you tell me some details?"

She looked down at him, her face completely expressionless.

"I will tell you what you are to do for me when we are together in your room."

"Well, see. . .I don't have all the special toys in my room. If you want something I don't have, I'd have to call down to get it sent up. It'd save time—and money—if we just—"

She moved, almost as fast as Quin, grabbed his arm and *yanked him* to his feet. The glass flew out of his hand, wine spilling out in an arc—

"Hey!"

"We are going to your room now," she said. "I have been patient long enough."

He planted his feet, but, honestly, he didn't think he could take her, and Patsy ought to—

"Where's my girl Jade?" A big voice demanded from the hallway.

"Three times a week I come here, and she's always waiting for me, with a big smile on her face. I 'spect to see her when I come in, 'less she's upstairs changin' into that *red dress* for me. No, no, I'll just take a looksee into the parlor, that's all. Might be somebody looking for some extra-big fun."

Villy heard a light step, and a big shadow came across the door.

"There you are!" yelled Cheever McFarland, and swung a long arm out to gather Villy in by the shoulders and tug him into a bear hug.

His captive arm—but she let him go, and turned all the way 'round to stare at Ms. Natesa, who was standing in the doorway to the back hall, gun steady in her hand, and her face closed and cold and somehow *still* more alive than his date's...

McFarland swung him behind his broad back—"Stay behind me, boy."—and *his* gun was out, too. Desa ven'Zel glanced at him over her shoulder, not looking particularly threatened, or the least little bit scared.

"You will come with us," Ms. Natesa said.

The other woman turned again to face her.

"I regret," she said—and gasped sharply.

McFarland swore and jumped forward, going down on one knee and catching her before she met the rug.

"Poison," he said, without looking up. He holstered his gun, and put a hand on her chest as she stiffened, making a sound like a kitten mewling, then collapsed, completely boneless.

"Dammit."

"Indeed."

Ms. Natesa slid her gun away, and came into the room.

"Villy, are you hurt?"

"No ma'am, just scareder than I ever been in my life."

"I regret that," she said, and paused, as if she heard the echo of Desa ven'Zel's last words.

"I am sorry that it took us so long to arrive. We needed to be certain that she was acting alone. You were very clever to keep her here in the parlor."

"She was getting ready to carry me up to my room," Villy said.

"Yes, we heard."

Cheever McFarland rose, Desa ven'Zel in his arms, and put her gently down on the sofa. Villy bit his lip, and looked over his shoulder gratefully as Ms. Audrey swept into the room.

She paused at his side, taking the situation in with one encompassing glance.

"I didn't hear a shot," she said, maybe to Ms. Natesa.

"She poisoned herself. We have learned that some of the operatives are equipped with this ability."

Audrey sighed, and turned to Villy.

"You all right, honey?"

"Yes, ma'am."

She gave him a close look.

"Just scared blue. Well. You and me and Patsy and Mr. Mc-Farland'll are gonna sit down, go over this and figure out how we could've handled this better. But not tonight. Tonight, I want you to take a drop and go to sleep."

He didn't usually take the sleeping drops, but he had a strong suspicion he wouldn't be doing any sleeping, unless he did. At least he didn't have the early shift at the Emerald tomorrow.

"Yes, ma'am," he said to Ms. Audrey, and she gave him another sharp look.

"I asked Teddy to keep you company tonight, all right?"

Teddy was old enough to be Villy's mother, he guessed. She was round and sharp-tongued and encompassing. He'd sleep good tonight, if Teddy was holding him, even without the drug.

Ms. Audrey must've seen that thought cross his face, 'cause she nodded, and said, "The drop too, Villy."

"Yes, ma'am," he said for a third time, and turned at another step in the hall, which was Teddy.

"Come on, honey," she said, opening her arms. "Let's get you comfy."

He nodded—and turned back to Ms. Audrey.

"I'm sorry about the wine on the new carpet," he said, wincing as he saw the red arc slashing through the field of pretty, pale flowers.

"Never you mind it," Ms. Audrey told him. "Mr. Luken tells me that rug's got a surface that'll repel anything. Just wipe it with a rag, he says. We'll test that in just a minute. Now, go to bed, Villy."

"Yes," he said, and nodded at the room. "Ms. Natesa. Mr. McFarland. Thank you."

Then he let himself be tucked under Teddy's arm and guided out of the parlor.

—end—

About The Authors

Maine-based writers **Sharon Lee and Steve Miller** teamed up in the late 1980s to bring the world the story of Kinzel, an inept wizard with a love of cats, a thirst for justice, and a staff of true power. Since then, the husband-and-wife have written dozens of short stories and twenty novels, most set in their star-spanning Liaden Universe®. Before settling down to the serene and stable life of a science fiction and fantasy writer, Steve was a traveling poet, a rock-band reviewer, reporter, and editor of a string of community newspapers. Sharon, less adventurous, has been an advertising copywriter, copy editor on night-side news at a small city newspaper, reporter, photographer, and book reviewer. Both credit their newspaper experiences with teaching them the finer points of collaboration. Sharon and Steve passionately believe that reading fiction ought to be fun, and that stories are entertainment. Steve and Sharon maintain a web presence at http://korval.com/

BOOKS by SHARON LEE & STEVE MILLER

The Liaden Universe

Fledgling

Saltation

Mouse and Dragon

Ghost Ship

Dragon Ship

Necessity's Child

Trade Secret

Dragon in Exile

Alliance of Equals

omnibus volumes

The Dragon Variation (Local Custom, Scout's Progress, Conflict of Honors)

The Agent Gambit (Agent of Change, Carpe Diem)

Korval's Game (Plan B, I Dare)

The Crystal Variation (Crystal Soldier, Crystal Dragon, Balance of Trade)

story collections

A Liaden Universe Constellation: Volume 1

THANK YOU

for your interest in
and support of
our work
—Sharon Lee and Steve Miller

Made in the USA
Columbia, SC
23 November 2017